My Monster

The Bully Buster

Boris To The Rescue

and

Felix The Naughty Monster

Kaz Campbell

Table of Contents

Story 1

Boris To The Rescue

Meet My Friend Boris

Can you imagine having a monster for a friend? Not a pretend monster, but a real one. I have to tell you it is AWESOME! This is my story of how I came to have a little red monster friend called Boris….

My name is Bob, my friends always call me Bobby. Mom and Dad call me Bob when I'm in trouble and Mom calls me *Boo Boo Bear* at home. This is really annoying and embarrassing, especially when my friends are around. After all, I'm in Grade 4 now, I'm almost a teenager!

Dad is a teacher at my school. His name is Mr. Campbell and the kids all really like him, except for Jack. Jack is a bully! Jack is not nice! And Jack gives me a hard time!

I have a secret friend called Boris. He says I am the best friend he has ever had! He makes me laugh and he looks after me, but sometimes he gets me into some strange situations. You see, most of the time, I am the only one who can see Boris and he is a real monster.

I think it is pretty special that nobody else can see

Boris. They can smell him and hear his noises (things like farts, hiccups and burps), but they can't hear him talking or see him. At first I told my best friends about Boris, but when they couldn't see him, they just looked at me and laughed.

I know you won't think I'm strange, so I'm going to tell you all about Boris...

Our First Meeting

We first met last year, when I was in Grade Three.

Every night I would have TERRIBLE dreams. Giant crabs would attack my toes with their giant claws. Little green aliens would abduct me from my bed and take me to their spaceship. Giant hairy spiders would drop from the ceiling and crawl onto my face. Scary monsters were hiding in my cupboard and would creep out at night and look at me. A huge dragon was under my bed. A witch would knock on the window and put a spell on me…turning me into a frog.

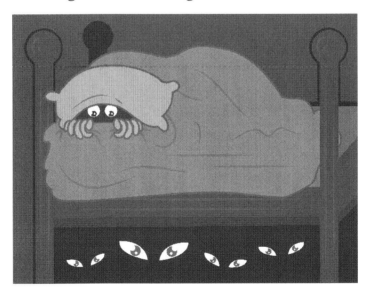

I had the same dreams every night and after every dream I would wake-up scared and hiding under the sheets. Sometimes I would scream for help and Mom would run in and hold me until I fell asleep again.

After school one day, Mom gave me a present. "Bobby this will help to stop your bad dreams, it is called a dream-catcher. We'll hang it above your bed tonight and it will catch all the scary things you dream about."

I just looked at Mom. How would something made of wool, beads and feathers catch a giant crab or stop a witch from knocking on my window?

"Thanks Mom, but I don't think it will work," I said hunching my shoulders and not looking forward to night time.

Mom told me it had special powers, very strong magical powers. "I'm sure it will work Boo Boo

Bear (I wish she would stop calling me that), let's just give it a try."

That night she tucked me into bed, read me a story and told me to ask the dream catcher to catch the scary dreams. Then she switched off the light and left me all alone.

I closed my eyes and repeated in my head, "Dream-catcher please work, dream-catcher please work...." And soon I fell asleep.

I heard a high-pitched creepy noise, it sounded like fingernails scraping down a blackboard. A dragon's claw started to slide out from under my bed. It was rough, scaly and huge! Its fingernails were scaping on the floor.

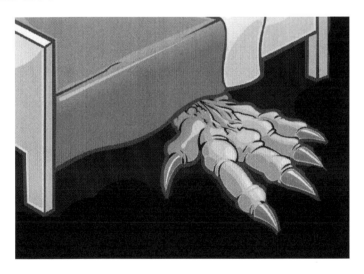

"Oh no, please help me dream-catcher," I cried. I looked at the catcher because I was too scared to look down and out of the dream-catcher jumped a red hairy monster.

I jumped up in bed, the little red monster was just above my head. It had a sword in one hand and a shield in the other. I felt sure it was going to slice my head off!

"Settle down Bobby, I'm here to help you, no need to scream…Boris to the rescue!" he said as he jumped down to the floor.

Suddenly the bed tilted and started to lift as the dragon roared and charged towards the little red monster. Fire poured from the dragon's mouth and nostrils. I felt for sure that the monster was toast. But the monster showed that he was tougher than a slice of bread and deflected the fire with his shield.

"Charge!" screamed the red monster as he ran flat out with the sword pointed straight at the dragon's snout. The dragon swished its tail and knocked the sword flying.

The monster and the dragon wrestled on the floor, they rolled across the room and the dragon hit the wall with a thud. While the dragon was dazed, the monster picked up his sword and with one swift slice he cut the dragon's head off.

Then he picked up the head and threw it out the window. The rest of the body turned to smoke and blew swiftly outside.

The little red monster was a hero. He had saved me from the dragon.

"Did you kill the dragon?" I asked.

The monster smiled, "No Bobby, it's not dead I've just sent it back to Dream Land and it won't ever come back again."

"Who, I mean, what are you?" I asked the monster.

"My name is Boris and I just saved you from a dragon dream, you can thank me if you want…" he said with a huge smile on his face.

"Ahh..thank you Boris, but you haven't answered my question, what are you?" I asked again.

"Bobby, I'm a friendly monster. I came from the dream-catcher and it is my job to look after you. So go back to sleep and never fear, Boris is here." And with that he did a funny little dance and hopped onto the end of my bed.

I pulled up the sheets and slept all night without another dream. In the morning as I woke up I saw Boris, the monster disappearing back into the dream-catcher.

The next morning I told Mom and she wanted to know all about my monster friend. Dad looked up from his breakfast and shook his head. I don't think Dad believes me, but Mom does.

And that is how Boris came into my life.

The Longest Day

At school that day I told my best friends, Kade and James, all about Boris. They thought it was really cool and wanted to meet Boris. So I decided that if Boris came back tonight I would ask him to come to school with me so he can meet my friends.

School that day seemed to take forever! My teacher, Mr. Eggerton talked for hours about how to write a letter and how to add up numbers. Didn't he know I had better things to think about? I couldn't concentrate and as I was drawing a picture of Boris...I felt a dark and cold presence behind me. The hairs on the back of my neck stood up and goosebumps appeared on my arms. You know, the type of feeling you have when you think a vampire is sneaking up on you.

As I started to turn I heard, "Bob, what are you doing?"

"Sorry Mr. Egghead, I mean Mr. Eggerton...I'm just drawing a picture of my monster, but I was listening to your interesting talk about how to write letters," I said in a voice that was high and way too fast.

He ripped the page out of my book, scrunched it up and threw it in the bin.

"Okay class, seeing that Bob HAS been listening, he is going to tell us how you finish a letter to a friend," he said, knowing he was setting me up for making a fool of myself.

Why didn't I listen when I was drawing? I could feel my face getting hotter and hotter. I mumbled, "Goodbye…"

Everyone started laughing. Everyone that is, except Mr. Eggerton. Looking around, I wished that the aliens would fly through the window and abduct me!

I knew what would come next. "I'll be seeing your Dad at lunchtime Bob, right after I give you a detention."

Sometimes it is painful having a Dad who teaches at the same school. I just slumped in my seat (trying to make myself invisible) and told him I was sorry and that I would listen from now on.

During detention I had to write out - *I will listen in class* –50 times before I could escape.

When I finally made it to the playground to join in the last 10 minutes of a soccer game, Jack the class bully, picked up the soccer ball and yelled, "How come you are out of detention, oh, that's right, Daddy is a teacher. Little Bobbly always gets special attention. Teacher's pet, teacher's pet, Bobby is the teacher's pet," he chanted.

Kade jumped to my defence, "Leave him alone Jack,

he did his detention."

"Yeah right, all 5 minutes of it, I'd be in there all lunch hour and so would all the other kids, teacher's little favorite!" he said in a mean voice.

Kade took the ball off Jack and yelled for everyone to play on. Jack gave me a death stare, so I just smiled at him and ran off after the ball. Sometimes you just have to ignore bullies. And I'm so lucky to have friends who stand up for me.

After lunch the day dragged on, I couldn't wait to go home!

Early To Bed

That night I did my homework quickly, ate all my dinner in record time, even the cabbage (yuck!), I didn't even try to hide my peas under the table, then I had a shower and cleaned my teeth…all before 6 o'clock.

"Mom, Dad, I'm really tired, I think I'll go to bed early tonight," I said trying to sound sleepy. My act was worthy of an academy award, I yawned and stretched and made my eyes look as if they were half closed.

My big sister, Lucy, looked at me with a strange look on her face and her arms folded. "But Bobby you never want to go to bed," she said in a shocked voice.

Mom and Dad looked surprised too. "Don't worry about today Bobby, Mr. Eggeton can't expect little kids to listen to every word he says and besides learning about how to write a letter is pretty boring," Dad tried to comfort me, thinking I was upset about getting into trouble at school. To be honest, I had forgotten all about it. I just wanted to go to bed to see Boris.

"Thanks Dad (yawn), I'm just tired (yawn), I'll see you in the morning," I replied.

Mom walked over and gave me a hug, she put her hand on my forehead to feel for a temperature. "Are you sure you feel okay? I'll come in and read you a story Boo Boo Bear (I hate that nickname) and sit with you until you fall asleep," whispered Mom.

Now normally, I would love that, but not tonight.

"It's okay Mom, I'm a big boy now…goodnight," and off I went to bed.

***

Lucy watched me walk up the stairs, "Mom, that's not normal, Bobby is up to something."

"I agree," said Dad. "Where are all his excuses for NOT going to bed? How come he doesn't suddenly have extra homework…why isn't he feeling thirsty or hungry and why didn't he want you to read with him tonight? Something is up," said Dad.

"Oh you two are so suspicious! He just feels tired and he is starting to grow up. I'm proud of our Bobby and I think the dream-catcher is making him feel safer in his room. I am one brilliant mom!" she boasted.

My New Best Friend

Tonight I jumped into bed, pulled up my blankets, looked at the dream-catcher and whispered, "Boris, hey Boris, it's okay to come out." And whamo, he appeared straight away with a big smile on his face.

Guess what? Boris likes to play games. He loves to play hide and seek! But boy is he hard to find, especially in my messy cupboards! We dressed up as pirates and played sword fights. Not with his steel sword, but with my plastic ones. It is just like having a brother, but one who doesn't argue with you.

Luckily I heard Mom coming up the stairs to check on me. Leaping into bed, I pulled the blankets up over my neck. I didn't want her to see my pirate outfit. She thought I was fast asleep and gave me a kiss on the cheek, "Goodnight my beautiful son, I love you."

Boris was sitting on my bed leaning against me watching her. He didn't hide! How could Mom not notice a red monster. My Mom sees EVERYTHING! And then she left and closed the door.

"Boris, why didn't you hide, Mom could have seen you," I whispered.

Boris jumped onto my tummy, "Don't stress Bobby, nobody sees me unless I show myself to them. You could say I'm invisible to everyone else but you."

"So nobody can see you except me!" wow, that was a lot to take in.

Boris looked me straight in the eye, "It is like this Bobby, you needed to see me. Your dreams were totally out of control. I'm here to help you."

"So I can take you anywhere and I'm the only one who can see you?" I asked.

"That's right buddy, I decide who sees me," he said looking rather smug.

"Would you please come to school with me Boris?" I pleaded, thinking about how much fun we could have. Boris agreed, but only on the condition that he stays invisible to everyone else and that included my best friends Kade and James. I felt disappointed that I wouldn't be able to show them Boris, but I was sure they would understand.

I have a feeling that school won't be so boring tomorrow and then I drifted off to sleep.

Boris Comes to School

This was going to be the most exciting day ever! I jumped out of bed, dressed quickly and scoffed down my breakfast.

Everyone in my family was looking at me strangely. "Excuse me, but WHO are you?" said Lucy (in her older sister…I'm suspicious of you) voice. Mom smiled and Dad raised his eyebrows and tilted his head, it was hard to fool my Dad.

Maybe I should explain that normally I go into

super slow motion when I am getting ready for school. Normally the neighbors listen to my parents calling out, "Hurry up Bob, I'm late…go and get dressed…eat your breakfast quickly…have you cleaned your teeth yet…where's your bag…don't forget your lunch box…have you packed your homework…put your shoes on…where's your hat" and these are just a few of the things they say EVERY morning.

"Just looking forward to school Lucy, what's wrong with that?" I said, trying to look innocent. I quickly walked back to my bedroom, closed the door and whispered into the dream-catcher, "Boris, come out, it is time to go to school."

I felt a slight breeze hit me in the face. It smelled bad, like rotten fish…and then Boris jumped out of the catcher.

"Yoo Bro, I can't wait for this. My Monster School is so boring, I've never seen a human school before. Are we going in your Dad's car?"

With my hands on my hips I shook my head, "No Boris, I have to maintain some degree of coolness, Dad and I keep our distance at school. "And with that we high-fived and walked out the door, past my family who still couldn't believe that I was going to school on time and without any nagging. We walked a couple of houses down to the bus stop.

Boris had never been on a bus. You would think he would be nervous, but no, Boris was like an excited tiger cub after a ball of wool. He ran to the back and jumped up onto the back seat smiling.

Luckily my house is the first bus stop. I quickly walked down and told Boris that we couldn't sit there.

"Why not?" asked Boris.

"Because this is where the cool tough kids sit, I'm not allow to sit here," I explained.

Boris looked thoughtful, "But Bobby you are cool and I am tough, so combined we can sit here," he tried to explain. Boris was going to get me killed before I even got to school. I tried to pull him off the seat and we were pulling back and forth, back and forth.

The bus driver, Sam, called out, "Are you okay Bobby?"

"Sure Sam, I'm…just doing some exercises," I replied. I'm going to have to be more careful or people will think I'm going crackers. I left Boris in the back seat and went to my normal seat towards the middle. He is just going to have to understand there are certain rules. The nerds sit up the front (as far away from the backseat as they can), the normal kids sit in the middle and the naughty and cool kids sit at the back of the bus. That is just the way things are.

As the bus started to fill, Boris could see that I was right, the back seat was definitely not a good place to be. Jack (the class bully) was sitting next to him, swearing and saying mean things about everyone as they got onto the bus. I turned around and had a quick look at Boris. He had a very grumpy look on his face, he wasn't happy.

"Hey Bobby Boo Boo Bear, teacher's pet, I'm your worst nightmare. You're going down today!" Jack yelled at me so that everyone on the bus could hear.

I pretended I couldn't hear him, but I could feel my heart racing and my face turning a bright shade of red. All the kids around me put their heads down…it is called trying to avoid being picked on. The kids at the back of the bus all laughed and the nerds (who were used to being bullied) just shook their heads.

Why did Mom have to still use that silly nickname, it was okay when I was one, but not 8! Jack heard her call me that at a Parent Day (about 2 years ago!!!) and he hasn't let me forget it.

"Aarrrrrrgh, who did that!" Jack yelled. I turned around and he had yoghurt dripping down off his head. At first there was stunned silence, then everyone on the bus, including the nerds, started laughing and cheering.

Boris walked up the aisle with a huge smile on his face. "That will teach him to be mean to you Bobby," he said as he licked yoghurt off his fingers.

Boris' First Day at Human School

Boris and I walked into class. Kade and James came running up to me, asking where Boris was.

"Sorry boys, Boris is doing something else today, maybe he'll come another day," I said, feeling bad for telling a lie. "You should have seen him last night, he is so much fun. We played pirates and hide and seek in my bedroom."

Kade and James looked at each other and smiled. James raised his eyebrows, "Sure Bobby, sure you're not going all loony on us," and he punched me in the arm.

"Boris is real boys, I promise that one day I'll let you meet him," I replied. But I could see that they weren't convinced.

"Stinky Jack" was sitting in front of me and boy did

he smell. I smiled as I imagined how smelly he would be by the end of the day as the yoghurt went off.

Mr. Eggerton always started the day off with a joke, "Where do pencils go on vacation…pencil-vania." Boris cracked up, he was rolling around the floor laughing his head off. Now the joke wasn't even funny, but Boris…watching him made me laugh out loud. I looked up and every head had turned in my direction. Kade whispered, "Are you okay Bobby?"

Mr. Eggerton smiled, "Finally someone gets my jokes." I didn't know what to say, so I just smiled and gave him a thumbs up.

Then everyone started laughing, except Jack, he mouthed, "Teacher's pet, you crawler," at me. I looked down at Boris and he was giving Jack a death stare.

"Okay everyone, enough fun for today, take out your math books and we'll start working," the teacher instructed, breaking the tension between Jack and myself.

"Yay," said Boris, "I love math!" I gave him an - *are you for real* - look. How could anyone love math!

Even though my Dad is a teacher, I am at best a C student and I really struggle with math and spelling. So when Boris said that he loves math, I was really happy as he could help me. We started off with the 3 times tables. Mr. Eggerton would call out a sum and we had to raise our hand to answer it. Now normally I never put my hand up because I often get the answers wrong, but today I had Boris to help me.

"3 X 7?" Boris called out 21 immediately, so I raised my hand. My teacher looked surprised, "Bobby…"

"21 Sir," I called out.

"Excellent Bobby, you must have been practicing at home," he said in a happy voice.

And this continued on, I was the first to raise my hand every time and I got every sum right! Having

Boris at school was definitely going to make me look smarter.

Then Mr. Eggerton put an addition sum on the blackboard and told us to work it out. Boris told me the answer straight away, so I raised my hand and gave the correct answer once again.

"That's amazing Bobby, how did you work that out so quickly?" he asked. "Come up to the blackboard and show your classmates how to work it out."

Oh no, I had NO idea! I wasn't listening yesterday! I didn't know how to do it! I could feel my face turning red, my hands were getting sweaty. I couldn't tell my teacher that the invisible red furry monster next to me had told me the answer.

I walked slowly to the front, dragging my feet. Boris could sense my fear. "Don't worry Bobby, I'll tell you how to do it," trying to make me feel better. And then Boris told me what to do and what to say. My teacher was amazed! The whole class was shocked! Who was this boy at the front of the classroom, surely not Bobby Campbell who is no good at math!

"Wow Bobby," said Mr. Eggerton, "you must have been listening yesterday."

I gave him a smile and returned to my seat. On the way, Jack stuck his foot out and tripped me. I went flying into the air and I fell flat on my bottom.

Then he jumped out of his seat and offered to help me get up. I just looked at him and shook my head. Of course, this was just an act for the teacher.

"So sorry Bobby, I didn't see you coming," he said with a smirk on his face.

I sat back down again. Boris had steam coming out of his ears. His little horns started twitching. He was so angry! "Don't let him get away with that Bobby!"

I couldn't answer him because I would look like I was talking to myself, so I just shrugged.

At recess I took Boris into the toilets so I could talk to him.

"Boris, sometimes kids are mean and Jack is always mean. I can't just fight him or tell him off every time he does something," I explained.

Boris was still fuming, "You have to do something Bobby, he is being so nasty to you."

"Boris, I know he is being nasty to me, but what can I do?" I yelled back.

"You can stand up for yourself Bobby, don't let him push you around!" he yelled back.

"What do you want me to do, bash him up!" I screamed, feeling frustrated and angry.

"Boys come out at once," called a loud and low voice.

Oh no, it's Mr. Stone, the school principal and he thinks there is someone else in here that I am talking to. What can I do?

"Come out now, both of you!" he yells again.

I wash my hands, trying to think of an excuse. Nothing comes to mind, how can I explain that I was arguing with an invisible little red monster? Maybe I can escape. Climb out the window (no too high), flush myself down the toilet (no, I'm too big and people do poos in there - yuck)...there was no way out. I took a deep breath and walked out.

"Hi, Mr. Stone, it was just me in there," I say, hoping that he buys my story.

"Don't lie to me Bob, who was in there with you?" he demanded.

"Honestly, it was just me," I reply. And with that he walks straight into the boys' toilets.

"Who else is in here, come out now!" Then he looks around, checking each toilet and realizes there is nobody else in there. "Are you okay Bob, you sounded like you were fighting, aahhhh, with yourself?"

"I'm fine Sir, I was just thinking out loud," I say, feeling embarrassed and knowing that he will tell my father. Great...now the principal thinks I'm going crazy too.

"Well Bobby, if you ever need anyone to talk to, you can come to my office anytime." He gave me an - *I feel sorry for you* - smile and walked off.

Boris Strikes Back

After lunch Mr. Eggerton always makes us read silently for 10 minutes. Sometimes I think he just wants to finish his coffee, but it is a nice quiet time in our classroom.

Boris sits next to me. His horns are twitching and he still has some smoke coming from his ears. This seems to happen whenever he is upset or angry. I give him a smile and start reading my book.

"Jack, can you clean off my board?" asks Mr. Eggerton. Jack hates reading, so he gladly hops up and starts cleaning off the board.

I look up from my book and Boris has disappeared. I look under my desk and all around the classroom and then I spot him, out the front standing close to Jack. Boris has a huge grin on his face and I wonder what he is up to.

Then I hear the longest and loudest fart I have ever heard. Boris is bending over with his bottom facing towards the class. Everyone looks towards the noise. Towards Jack! His face goes bright red and he starts to shake his head.

"It wasn't me," Jack says in a high-pitched voice.

Then Boris gives me a wink and bends over again. He lets out another fart that matches Jack's voice…very long and very high pitched.

"That wasn't me either," Jack yells, as his face turns purple.

All my classmates have now recovered from the shock and burst into laughter. James in laying on the floor, rolling around laughing. The girls are giggling and some of them have tears running down their cheeks from laughing so hard. Even Mr. Eggerton is laughing.

"Okay everyone (laugh), settle down (laugh), it is only air (laughing louder)," he blurted out. Mr. Eggerton was barely holding himself together.

Then a smell started to slowly spread across the room. Not a nice smell, but the worst fart smell you can imagine. It was like a cloud of poo and rotten fish. It was DISGUSTING! The laughter stopped, everyone slapped their hands over their mouths and noses.

Mr Eggerton's face turned red at first and then it started to turn green. The poor man, he was standing very close to Boris.

"Get out everyone, save yourself!" yelled Mr. Eggerton. And then he threw-up. Vomit erupted from his mouth like a raging volcano. This made the smell and yuck factor much worse! Sarah, who sits down the front, took one look at Mr. Eggerton and she threw-up as well, all over her desk. It was easy to see what she had for lunch.

We all raced towards the door, still holding our noses. Children were vomiting in the bushes outside the room. It was chaos.

Once outside I took in a huge breath. Oh how sweet

the fresh air was.

And then, while everyone was lying on the grass recovering, Jack said in a quiet voice, "It wasn't me."

My classmates just stared at him. Mr. Eggerton said, "Jack, you probably should go to the toilet."

Jack went bright red and yelled, "I said it wasn't me, Mr. Eggerton!"

Even Jack's bully friends started making snide comments like, "Sure Jack, we believe you, not!"

Jack walked off in a huff towards the toilet.

Boris came out of the classroom looking really proud of himself. I gave him a smile. "Now that is how you handle a bully, Bobby. I love payback time!" and he started laughing. I just shook my head at Boris and thought…how can one little monster cause so much trouble.

The smell inside was so bad that we couldn't go back in all afternoon. Instead we went to the oval and played sport. So Boris not only embarrassed Jack, the biggest meanest bully I've ever met, but he also got us some more sport time. Outstanding farting Boris! It is just a pity that so many of my classmates felt sick from the smell.

On the bus trip home Jack was VERY quiet! He sat up the front, giving the nerds a bit of a fright to begin with, but then they realized he was just hiding from his "friends".

One of the nerds tried to talk to Jack, "I say man, pretty awesome farting."

Jack started to stand, his chest puffed out and his fists clenched into balls. But then he sat back down again and pulled his hat over his face. "Don't talk to me, nerd," he said in a mean voice.

I could see all the kids at the front of the bus smiling. As they got off the bus, every single one of them called out in a loud voice, "Bye Jack, see you tomorrow." And every time one of the nerds called out goodbye, Jack slunk lower into his seat.

***

When we got home, I asked Boris if he would like something to eat.

"Yeah Bobby, I'm starving," Boris replied. "Do you have any tuna or pickles?" he asked.

So that is why Boris' breath smells so bad.

"Sure Boris, how about a tuna and pickle sandwich?" Boris greedily ate the sandwich, he ate it in one big mouthful and chewed with his mouth open. Bits of tuna fell onto his red fur. When he swallowed the sandwich with a huge gulp, he quickly licked the tuna off his fur and then slapped his lips together making a slurping noise.

"Best sandwich ever, Bobby," Boris said and then he let out a huge burp. It went for about 5 seconds and it smelt like rotten fish. I backed away, afraid I would vomit.

Mom must have heard Boris burp, she called out, "Are you okay Bobby, are you sick, honey?"

"No Mom, I'm fine," I called back.

And then Mom walked into the kitchen. "Bobby that smell is disgusting, was that you burping?"

"No Mom, Boris burped after he ate a tuna and pickle sandwich," I replied, wondering what her reaction would be.

Mom looked at me with her serious look and then she broke into a smile and on her way out of the room she stopped and said, "Bobby, you are such a joker, now clean up this mess and get on with your homework."

Boris helped me with my homework (he is really good at math). He has a super quick math brain, he is like a high powered calculator.

We started playing some Xbox games. Boris got upset and he started crying. He is very loud when he cries and orange snot started running down from his nose.

I asked him, "What is wrong, Boris?"

"Why did you kill the monster, Bobby?" he asked.

"Sorry Boris, let's play another game," I said. I think I'll give that game away.

It was then that the wall behind my bed started to shake. We heard crying, it was followed by a call for help. Boris and I looked at each other. And then the screaming became much louder and scarier. It was coming from the dream-catcher!

A little green monster appeared in my dream-catcher.

"Help! HELP! Aaarrrrrrhhhh!!!!! And then he was pulled back into the hole and disappeared.

"What is it Boris?" I was scared too.

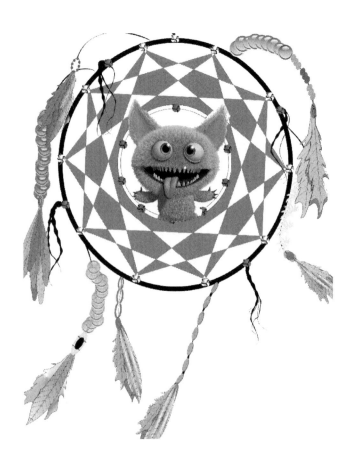

"It is my little brother Felix, he needs me! He must be in great danger!" cried Boris as he sprang to his feet and ran to the dream-catcher. And with that terrible news, Boris dived into the dream-catcher and disappeared.

Story 2

Felix The Naughty Monster

The Creepy Crawly Spider

I sat on my bed staring at the dream-catcher. There was NO way I was going to get to sleep tonight. I was too worried about Boris' little brother! What had happened? Was Boris okay? Who had pulled Felix into the hole and why was he so scared?

Three hours later and still no word from Boris. My eyelids were getting very heavy and everything looked blurry. Had that really happened or was I dreaming again?

Maybe the fumes from Boris' fart and his tuna and pickle burp were making me imagine things! I slid into bed, trying to keep my eyes from shutting. As I pulled up my sheets, I closed my eyes (just for a moment) and drifted off to sleep.

That was when I felt something round and hairy jump onto my face. OH NO! The spider dream was back. I hate this dream. A big spider swings down from the roof onto my face and then it bites me.

It's only a dream, it's only a dream…I tell myself. And then I feel the spider open its mouth. I can feel the wetness of its mouth on my face and then it kisses me. The spider just kissed me!

Sitting up quickly, I turn on the bedside lamp. The spider is sitting on my lap, looking at me. It is bright pink and hairy and has teeth. I pick up a book to squash the weird looking spider. I swing it back over my head and try to bring it down. But the book just stays in mid-air. Trying with all my power I can't pull it down, so I let the book go and it just sits above my head.

Now I'm not sure which is freaking me out the most, the pink spider or the book above my head. Slowly I turn my head to see why the book is stuck and I see Boris' arm holding the book as he is coming out of the dream-catcher above my bed.

"Boris!" squealed the pink spider.

"It's okay Trixie, Bobby thought you were a spider, he won't hurt you," Boris said in a soft and caring voice.

"So Bobby, you have met my little sister, Trixie."

"That's your sister, but she doesn't have any arms or legs or horns," I spluttered.

Boris smiled at Trixie, "That is because she is a baby monster, she is only one year old, we don't grow arms and legs until we are five and the horns don't grow until we are 13."

I put my opened hand out to Trixie. "I'm sorry Trixie, I thought you were a spider that I often dream about," I explained.

"That's okay Bobby, Boris told me all about you. Boris likes you and so do I," she replied. She was so sweet and cute, lucky that Boris held onto the book!

Trixie jumped up onto my hand. Her fur was so soft and tickly. I carefully passed her to Boris. He gave her a kiss and put her back into the dream-catcher. "Off you go Trixie, you know you are too young to come into Human Land." She smiled and jumped back into the dream-catcher.

"That was a close call Boris," I breathe a sigh of relief.

And then I remembered how Boris had gone to the rescue of Felix the night before. "What happened to your little brother Felix, is he okay?"

"He is fine Bobby. He was being very naughty at Monster Preschool, throwing a huge tantrum because he wasn't chosen for a reward. You see Felix isn't very smart…not like me…he struggles at school. He worked really hard on a project and he was sure that his teacher, Mr. Dumbleweed, would like it. But when Mr. Dumbleweed was handing out the fried cockroaches (they are like candy to monsters), Felix didn't get one. He started crying and screaming that it wasn't fair. Nobody could control him and then he blew huge amounts of orange snot into his hands and threw it all over Mr. Dumbleweed. It was all over his fur. Bright orange snot!"

"Mr. Dumbleweed almost exploded! He chased after Felix. They ran all around Monster Land. Felix is a fast runner, but so is his teacher. Then Felix decided to jump into the dream-catcher to get me to help him."

"When I jumped through, Mr. Dumbleweed had Felix by the feet, he was holding Felix upside down and telling him in a very angry voice that he was a "naughty little monster."

"That was when our mom and dad arrived. Dad was really angry with Felix and he told him that he isn't allowed to eat any of his favorite foods for a whole week. Mom banned him from watching his favorite movie Monsters Inc. So now Felix is feeling really sad."

Boris looked sad too.

"We are hoping he will stop his naughty ways when he grows horns. You see, monsters are different to human kids. When human kids turn 13, they grow invisible horns and become very naughty. Monster kids grow horns at 13 too, but that is when we stop being naughty and grow-up."

"I'd love to meet Felix, can he visit?" I asked Boris hopefully.

"He would love to get to know you Bobby, but I'm warning you, he is TROUBLE!" Boris said in a serious voice. "He is the same age as you Bobby, but he is really naughty!"

"Bobby you had better get some sleep, school is on tomorrow and I can't wait to go with you again."

"Good night Boris, I can't wait either," I said as I closed my eyes and fell back to sleep.

Boris The Genius

The bus trip to school today was much better. Boris sat next to me and left the back seat to the cool kids. Jack sat up the front again, with his hood pulled over his head. He had a really grumpy look on his face and he was all hunched over. Everyone ignored him today. Even the nerds could see that he was in a **dangerous** mood.

My classroom was almost back to normal, the smell of Boris' fart and the teacher's vomit had almost disappeared. If you breathed deeply, you could still smell a whiff of Boris' fart.

I unpacked my books and set them out on my table. Jack stomped in, walked up to my desk and swiped everything off my desk onto the floor. "Don't look at me Boo Boo Bear!" he quietly growled.

I looked at Boris, steam was starting to pour out and he didn't look happy. Quickly I mouthed, **"NO!"** Boris folded his arms and sat down, still steaming.

I picked up my books just as Mr. Eggerton started the class.

"Morning class, hope you are all feeling better today," he said with a smile. Let's start the day with a joke…"

"What did one toilet say to another toilet…You look a little flushed."

And he burst into laughter.

So did Boris. Once again he thought Mr. Eggerton's joke was hilarious and he totally cracked-up. I couldn't help myself and I also burst into laughter. Not at the joke, but at Boris rolling around laughing.

Jack turned around and in his meanest and quietest voice, he whispered, "Toilet jokes are **NOT** funny."

I just looked at him, "What?" I said.

"You're just laughing because of what happened yesterday," he growled.

To be honest, at first I had no idea what he was talking about and then it clicked. "Well, Jack, your fart was pretty funny and really stinky," I whispered back.

"It wasn't me! I hate you Bobby Boo Boo Bear," he said with a face full of rage.

"I don't really like you either Jack," I said in a moment of insanity. Why did I say that? I must have gone insane!

Luckily for me, Mr. Eggerton called out, "Jack and Bobby stop talking, okay class get out your math books."

Phew…saved by my math book! Never thought I'd say that.

"Way to go Bobby, that's my boy, don't let that bully push you around!" said Boris punching into the air and doing a triple backflip.

I looked at him and raised my eyebrows. Boris didn't realize that I had just caused myself a LOT of trouble.

***

Once again Boris helped me with the answers. I was on fire! The answers flew off my tongue. Mr. Eggerton was really happy with me and told me he would be telling my Dad about how much I had improved.

To be honest, I don't really want him to tell Dad because I know Dad will quiz me at home and if Boris isn't around, I'll get everything wrong.

"No need to do that Mr. Eggerton," I replied, hoping he wouldn't report to Dad.

The bell rang for recess and Boris and I headed out for a snack. I had packed some pickles in my lunchbox for Boris and he took them out when my friends weren't watching and gobbled them up.

English class was next. Did I tell you that I'm not very good at spelling? Actually, I totally suck at spelling! It doesn't seem to matter how much I practice, I always get the words wrong. As soon as my teacher says the words – spelling test – I break into a sweat, my hands shake and I feel really stressed. And today was Friday. Yes, you guessed it, SPELLING TEST DAY!

I ruled my book up, ready for this week's words.

"The first word is school," called out my teacher.

"Psst, Bobby, that's not how you spell it, it is S C H O O L," whispered Boris. Why he was whispering I don't know, nobody else could hear him. ☺

I changed the word on my book. From then on, Boris told me how to spell all the words. Mr. Eggerton collected the books to mark and gave me an – *I know you're hopeless at spelling* look.

While he was marking our tests, we had to write about our best friend. I wrote about Boris. I showed Boris and he thought it was really cool and he beamed with happiness.

"Bobby Campbell come to my desk," called Mr. Eggerton. Everyone stopped writing and looked at me. My face went red and I started to panic.

"Dumbo," whispered Jack.

I shook my head at Boris, warning him not to do anything to Jack. And I started the walk of dread to the teacher's desk, letting out a big sigh when I got there.

"Congratulations Bobby, I never thought you

would get 10 out of 10 for your spelling test. Well done son!" he said in a loud voice.

I stood there in shock. Normally I would get 2 or 3 right. I think the whole class was in also in shock at first and then they all started clapping. Boris jumped up onto Mr. Eggerton's desk and started dancing and singing to *We Are The Champions*.

At first this felt great, but then I realized that I had really cheated. I didn't get 10 out of 10, Boris did.

I mumbled a thank you to Mr. Eggerton and returned to my seat. Boris followed behind me doing the cha-cha dance.

Jack called out, "Mr. Eggerton, I think Bobby was cheating off me."

My teacher's reply was stern, "No Jack, he didn't, you only got 6 right."

On the way home in the bus, Ally sat next to me. She is a really nice girl in my class who lives next door.

"Wow Jack, that spelling mark was amazing, you should be so happy with yourself," she said smiling.

Now I felt even guiltier. A huge load was on my back!

"Thanks Ally, but I guessed most of them, it really is no big deal," I said, trying to play it down.

Boris was in my ear, "Bobby she likes you, talk to her, tell her how nice she looks… say this – Ally, you are beautiful, your eyes shine like diamonds and your smile is like the sun, your breath smells of sweet flowers on a windy day – go on Bobby," he urged.

I smiled and tried to ignore Boris. When we got back to my bedroom he was pacing the floor, "You are so chicken Bobby, why didn't you tell her that you like her, why didn't you tell her that she is beautiful?"

"Boris I'm only 8! Kids don't talk like that and she probably doesn't like me anyway!" I explained.

"Of course she likes you Bobby, you are the coolest and smartest kid in the class! Besides you need to find a wife soon, you are only 6 years away from turning 14! And 14 is the perfect age to get married!"

"14! Nobody gets married at 14!" I laughed.

"Monsters get married at 14…how old are you going to be when you get married Bobby," Boris asked seriously.

"At least 30 or maybe even 40," I replied, shaking my head. "Monster Land is different to here, Boris. 8 year old kids don't think about getting married."

"Oh," said Boris, scratching his head.

My head dropped and I sighed, "Boris, I feel bad about letting you help me with my schoolwork, it isn't right. From now on just let me answer the questions, even if I get them wrong," I said.

Boris looked at me with a funny look on his face and shook his head, then he returned to the girlfriend talk.

"Okay Bobby, I won't help you with schoolwork, but can I help you with girl stuff?" he asked.

To be honest, I didn't want him to help me with girl stuff, but he was so cute, I couldn't say no. "All right Boris…do you want to play a sword fight?" And we played pirates until we were both too tired to play anymore.

Truth Time

Dad came home from work feeling really happy and that night as we sat down to dinner I found out why.

"Everyone, I want to tell you some good news," he started. "Mr. Eggerton came to see me after school today and he is very impressed with Bobby. Congratulations son, I'm so proud of you, he told me that you got 10 out of 10 for spelling."

"It's nothing Dad, just a few lucky guesses," I mumbled. But he hadn't finished…

"And you are the first to answer all the math questions in class AND you are getting them all right!" he sounded so happy.

"Oh Bobby, I am so proud of you too," Mom gushed.

"Did you cheat?" asked Lucy.

Mom and Dad gave her a filthy stare. "Don't be so rude Lucy!" said Mom.

I couldn't take it any longer. I had to confess. "Lucy is kind of right Mom and Dad, I had some help," I said feeling bad.

Dad asked who had helped me. Now this was going to be tricky.

"Boris helped me with the answers," I confessed.

"Is he new in your class?" asked Dad.

"Well, yes…okay here goes, Boris is the little red monster who comes out of my dream-catcher to help me with my bad dreams. He likes to come to school with me and he is really smart. But it is okay, I've told him that he is not allowed to tell me the answers anymore," I explained.

Lucy started laughing and almost choked on the food in her mouth. Mom just looked at me and gave a tight smile and Dad shook his head.

"Can Boris come with me to high school, I need help with Science," Lucy managed to blurt out between laughing and choking.

"Don't be mean, Lucy! Bobby, tell us more about Boris," Mom said.

I started, "Well he has red fur, horns and he is almost as tall as me."

"Enough, Bobby," said Dad. "You are just making up stories, there are no such things as monsters. Tell us the truth, who has been helping you!" The room fell silent, even Lucy had stopped laughing.

"It's okay, Bobby, just tell us, you won't get into trouble. It is better to tell us everything now," said Mom.

I didn't know what to say. I was telling the truth, but nobody believed me. Not even Mom…the lady who asks the angels for a good car parking space.

"Boris helps me and he is a real monster," I blurted out.

Lucy started giggling again. "Okay Bobby, we believe you. So when do we get to meet this little monster friend of yours?" she asked.

This was going to be hard to explain. "I am the only one who can see Boris because he is invisible."

Lucy smiled, "This just keeps getting better!" My big sister was really enjoying watching me squirm in my seat.

"Boris decides who gets to see him, but you can hear his farts and burps. Mom, remember yesterday when you heard that long burp sound…that was Boris, not me," I explained.

"And Boris throws all your toys all over the floor and makes a mess in the kitchen after school," said Lucy. She was really loving this.

"Be quiet, Lucy," said Dad. "Bobby, it sounds like you have invented this monster to cover for you when you do naughty things."

"NO Dad, HONEST! He is REAL!" I yelled, feeling angry that nobody was believing me.

"Calm down everyone, let's eat our dinner and Bobby if you want, we can talk about Boris later," said Mom.

Nobody believes me. Sometimes I wish Boris wasn't invisible.

Help Me, Boris

Mom took me to bed and read me a story called, 'The Boy Who Cried Wolf'. It was all about a boy who kept telling lies, until nobody believed him…which means she thinks I am telling lies!

"Thanks for the story, Mom, but Boris is real," I said as she kissed me goodnight.

I tried to stay awake, I wanted to talk to Boris. But my eyes got sleepier and sleepier and I fell asleep before he came.

***

Knock, knock, knock…there was someone knocking on my window. I looked up and I saw a witch.

"Bobby Bobby Bobby Boo, I shall put a spell on you. Green and slimy you will be…toil and trouble, spit and poo, turn into a frog, Bobby Bobby Boo," said the witch and then she pointed her finger at me.

I looked down, my skin was turning green. My legs were getting shorter and shorter and skin was growing between my toes! My tummy was becoming round and fat, it looked like a balloon. And then I tried to call out for help, but all that came out was…"ribbit."

Then the witch commanded, "Go and live in the duck pond, Bobby the Frog!" And she laughed and flew away on her broomstick.

I was spinning out of control and then…

I landed in a pond.

Swimming to the top, I gulped in some air and then called out to Boris.

"Boris ribbit, help ribbit, me ribbit!" I croaked.

All the other frogs in the pond laughed at me, "You silly frog, who is Boris?"

And then I could feel a hand on my shoulder. I screamed, "Leave me alone!" I closed my froggy eyes, I was too scared to look. Had the witch come back to turn me into something else?

And then I heard, "Never fear, Boris is here." "Don't worry Bobby, I'll take you home now. First I'll turn you back into a boy." He called out, *"Frog be gone!"* I looked at my skin, it was turning back from green to a pinky color. Then my legs stretched out and my toes were no longer webbed.

"Thanks Boris, you saved me again," I said hugging him.

Then I opened my eyes and I was in bed with Boris sitting next to me. "Wow, that was a bad dream Bobby," Boris said.

"Ribbit, ribbit," I said.

"Bobby! What's wrong?" Boris panicked.

"Got you!" I laughed, giving Boris a huge high 5. Boris smiled and ruffled my hair.

"Bobby I can't wait for school today, I love school," he said with an excited voice.

I laughed, "Not today Boris, it is Saturday and school is closed on Saturday and Sunday."

Boris slumped his shoulders and gave out a big sigh. He was very disappointed.

I slapped him on the back, "Don't worry Boris, we can play pirates today and hide and seek in the backyard, it is going to be so much fun."

My monster looked a little happier. "And on Sunday I am going to Ally's birthday Party and I want you to come too," I said.

"A Birthday Party, YAHOO!" he yelled. I LOVE parties. This is going to be so much fun. Will they have party hats? Will there be birthday cake? What about pin-the-tail on the donkey?"

"Slow down Boris…I'm sure it will be lots of fun and going with you will make it even more special," I said.

"OH NO, Bobby, I just remembered. I have to monster-sit my baby brother tomorrow…I won't be able to come." And then Boris started to cry, not little tears and quiet crying, but huge loud sobs and bucket loads of tears.

I felt so sorry for him. "Boris, why don't you bring your little brother, Felix to the party?" I asked, thinking how clever I was to have solved the problem.

"Do you mean it, Bobby, do you really mean it…I can still come and bring Felix with me…oh Bobby, you are the best kid ever!" he cried as he wrapped his arms around me and wiped his snot on my shoulder.

"I'm sure Felix will be a good monster, Bobby. I'll tell him that he isn't to get up to any naughty monster business." And then Boris started dancing around my bedroom, "We're going to a party, we're going to a party…."

We played pirate sword fights in my bedroom and then went outside and played in the backyard. Boris was so hard to find, even with his bright red fur! I searched for him for about an hour, until he gave me a huge clue. A really bad smell (just like the classroom smell) drifted across the backyard and it came from the back garden. As I walked towards the tomato bushes, the smell got stronger and stronger.

"Got you!" I called. There was Boris sitting in the garden eating vegetables! Uugghh! He was eating broccoli, tomatoes and beans. Yuck! "Why are you eating vegetables Boris, nobody likes vegetables!!!!"

Boris smiled, he had green things in his teeth.

"I love vegetables Bobby, pickles are my favorite food, then broccoli, then beans, then brussel sprouts, then cabbage…"

"Okay I get the picture Boris, you actually do like vegetables," I said, thinking that this could come in handy at the dinner table.

When the sun started to set, Mom called me in to have a bath and Boris went home through the dream-catcher to tell Felix about the party.

This had been the best day ever! And tomorrow was going to be even more fun!

The Birthday Party

On Sunday mornings I like to sleep-in. But this Sunday morning was going to be different. I was having a nice dream about playing soccer when I felt one of my eyelids open. Out of my eye I could see green fur. Something was holding my eyelid open.

"Wakey wakey, rise and shine Bobby, we've got a party to go to," said the little green monster.

"Felix, I told you not to do that. Bobby will wake up when he is ready," I could hear Boris say.

Was this a dream?

I opened my other eye and I could see Boris and Felix sitting on my bed watching me. Both of them had huge toothy grins on their faces. I looked at my clock…it was only 6am!

"Hi Boris, hi Felix," I said in a very sleepy voice.

Felix started bouncing up and down on my bed. "We're going to a party, we're going to a party…" he sang as he jumped.

Boris looked embarrassed, "Settle down Felix, otherwise Bobby won't take you to the party!"

Felix stopped jumping, "I'm sorry Bobby, I'll be good, I promise I'll be good, please let me go." And then he jumped off the bed and started putting my toys away in my toy box.

I felt sorry for the little monster. "Felix, stop working and tell me all about yourself," I said in a kind voice.

He jumped back onto my bed. "I thought you'd never ask Bobby, let's see"…and he pulled out a list of things about Felix.

All About Felix...

I am 8 years old.

I am very handsome.

I am good at tricking.

All the girls like me!

I have the BEST farts!

I love broccoli.

I love my big brother.

I am not smart like Boris.

I get into trouble at school sometimes.

I want to have my own human friend.

"Wow Felix, you are one cool monster. All except the part about loving broccoli! YUCK!!!!" and I pulled a face to show my hate of that vegetable.

I left Boris and Felix to play pirates and went downstairs to have breakfast.

Mom and Dad like to clean the house up on Sunday mornings, so I started on my chores to get them out of the way. I was dusting the lounge room when I heard Mom yell, "Bobby get up here now!"

Now my Mom is really nice and she doesn't normally yell, so I knew something was up. And then I remembered…Boris and Felix were in my room. I raced up the stairs as quickly as I could and ran into my room. It was almost destroyed. All my clothes were all over the floor. The sheets and blankets were totally off my bed. Every drawer had been tipped out. My toys were scattered everywhere.

Boris and Felix were sitting on my bed looking guilty.

"Bobby Campbell, get into your room right now and CLEAN UP THIS MESS!" Mom looked really mad. "I don't know what has got into you Bobby," and she turned and walked away, closing the door behind her.

I shook my head at the monsters, "Boris, Felix, what have you done?"

"We are so sorry Bobby, we were playing pirates and having so much fun and we got carried away," Boris said looking sad.

"But it was fun!" said Felix with a smile on his face.

"Well guys, let's see how much fun you have cleaning up this mess," I replied with a cross look on my face. I sat on the bed and folded my arms. "Hurry up, Mom will be back soon to check on me."

Boris and Felix went into super fast action. Monsters can move much faster than humans and within 10 minutes my room was perfect. Then we sat on the floor and I read a book to the monsters. They loved listening to a story about dragons.

"Dragons live in the next town to Monster Land, right behind the Fairy Kingdom. I don't like dragons, Bobby, they scare me when they breathe fire," said Felix in the cutest little voice.

"What does Monster Land look like?" I asked. I had no idea about my monster friends' home, school or family.

Boris looked very excited, "Oh Bobby, you would love Monster Land. We live in a forest and our house is built high in a tree."

"You live in a tree-house…wow, that sounds like so much fun Boris," I said, hoping he would tell me more.

"Do all the monsters look like you two?"

Boris smiled, "No Bobby, there are all types of monsters in Monster Land. But everyone in my family looks similar, we all have fur, but we are different colors."

"I'd love to visit your home one day, do you think that is possible Boris?" I asked.

"Of course you can, Bobby!" Felix jumped in. "You can share my bed, but not my toothbrush. You'll have to bring your own toothbrush," he said with a serious look on his face.

Boris shook his head, "It isn't that easy Bobby, I'll have to ask the King of Monster Land first. A human has never come to our home Bobby, you would be the first one."

Wow, imagine being the first person to go to Monster Land!

"Bobby, is that room tidy yet?" called out Mom. She walked into my room, "That is much better, Bobby, you had better get dressed for Ally's party, some of her friends are starting to arrive."

Felix did back-flips across the bedroom floor and Boris gave a huge grin. This was going to be the best birthday party ever.

***

Ally had asked me to perform a magic trick at her party. I quickly dressed and found my magician outfit, magic hat, rabbit and wand. I'm pretty good at pulling a toy rabbit out of a hat.

We walked next door to the party. Ally's parents had decorated the house and her Mom had baked a beautiful birthday cake. As the kids arrived, they put their presents in the corner and went outside to play.

Ally's Mom had made lots of yummy things to eat and most of it was really sweet. Except for one plate that had pickles, salami and cheese. When Boris and

Felix saw that plate, they both rushed over and helped themselves. They ate everything on the plate very quickly. Luckily nobody was watching or they would have seen pieces of food flying into the air and then disappearing!

Boris and Felix spotted a trampoline, "Monsters love to jump Bobby. Can we have a go?" Felix asked. I nodded yes and they ran over and started jumping.

My friends had all arrived and they loved my magician outfit. Ally said she couldn't wait to see my disappearing rabbit trick again (she must have seen it at least 20 times already). "You're such a great magician Bobby," she said in a sweet voice.

Boris called out to me, "Woohoo, see Bobby, I told you she likes you!" as he did a double backflip on the trampoline. I just smiled.

And that was when I noticed that Boris was on the trampoline by himself. Felix wasn't with him. I couldn't see him anywhere.

"Okay everyone, let's go inside and play *Pin The Tail On The Donkey*," called Ally's Mom.

Everyone cheered and ran inside. That is when I saw Felix. He had unwrapped all of Ally's gifts. They were scattered all over the floor.

Ally stopped and looked at the mess.

"Who did this?" she asked in a sad voice.

Total silence. Kids were shaking their heads. Nobody, except me (and my two monsters), knew what had happened.

I stepped forward, "It is okay Ally, you go and play the game and I'll pick your presents up for you and clean up the mess."

Ally and her Mom smiled at me, "Thanks Bobby, you're the best."

Boris winked at me and Felix tried to slink away towards the game. Boris picked him up and put him back near the mess he had made. "Clean it up Felix and no more trouble from you!"

"But it's not fair, I never get ANY presents and she

got 20!!!" screamed Felix. And then he started to cry. Did I say cry, I should have said that he had a huge super tantrum. He was wailing! This must be a monster thing!

"It's okay Felix, I'm not angry at you," I whispered, hoping that nobody would see me *talking to myself.*

He jumped up from the floor, grinned at me and said, "Thanks Bobby...I really like you."

***

"Over here everyone, Bobby is going to do his famous magic trick for us," called Ally.

I felt a little shy, my magic trick wasn't all that good. All I did was use an almost invisible fishing line to pull a toy rabbit out of a hat.

"Thank you everyone. Today I have my magic hat. This hat has great powers. With this wand, hat and some special magic, I am going to pull an animal out of this hat and then I shall make it disappear."

"Abracadabra, mice on the moon, watch this way, an animal will appear soon," and then I swished the wand through the air and lifted it away from the hat. Out of the hat popped Felix! And all the kids were clapping, cheering and jumping with excitement. They could see him! He must have shown himself to them! I looked down at him, just as he poked his tongue out.

"And now friends I will make the green monster disappear," and I tapped the wand on the hat and Felix disappeared.

Everyone was amazed. I was a star! "More, more, more," they chanted.

I bowed, "That is all for today, my name is Bobby Campbell, master magician of the universe."

Ally came forward and looked in the hat. She pulled out the toy rabbit and held it high. Everyone laughed and cheered again. "How did you do it Bobby?" they all asked.

"Sorry folks, a true magician never tells," I said with my chest puffed out. I looked over at Boris and Felix. Boris gave me the thumbs up and Felix took a huge bow.

***

"Birthday cake time," called out Ally's Mom. Everyone *oohed* and *aahed* at the cake, it looked beautiful! We sang happy birthday to Ally. Boris and Felix joined in…monsters have terrible singing voices!

And then it was time to blow out the candles. Ally was making a wish when the candles all went out at once. I looked over at Felix, but he was just standing there with his mouth closed.

Ally's Mom lit the candles again and as Ally started to bend over to blow them out, they went out again!

This time I had a whiff of pickles. I frowned at Felix, "It wasn't me Bobby, I promise," he said. Then I looked at Boris, he grinned and shrugged his shoulders.

As the candles were lit again, I looked from one monster to the other. My arms crossed and looking really grumpy. This time, Ally got to blow the candles out. Everyone cheered and called out,

"Happy Birthday Ally!"

Then a squeaky noise, like a balloon losing air, became louder and louder. It was followed by the most disgusting smell ever. Oh no, one of them had farted!

Everyone looked at each other, then they held their noses and ran outside. Everyone that is, except for Felix (yes it was Felix who had dropped this fart bomb).

Kids were rolling around the ground, trying not to be sick. Ally's parents were horrified! Then everyone started trying to work out who did it. I didn't get the blame because I wasn't near Felix, but Ally and Sam were the prime suspects! We all started laughing and after a while we went back inside, trying to ignore the smell.

Someone had bitten into the birthday cake! Gross!!!!

This was just too much for Ally and she burst into tears. I felt so bad for her. I had ruined her birthday party by bringing along two monsters.

Felix had disappeared. Naughty little monster!!!! "I'm so sorry Bobby," said Boris, he had tears coming down his face. I smiled at him and mouthed, *'It's okay Boris.'*

Mike, the coolest boy in our class, started laughing. Everyone just looked at him. And then he broke the tension, "This has been the BEST birthday party I have EVER been to!"

All the kids agreed and started laughing. "Well, I suppose it wasn't boring," said Ally in a cheeky voice.

"It wasn't boring, it was the BEST!" yelled Mike and everyone agreed.

***

We all went outside for Ally to look at her presents. It was still too smelly inside. Most of the girls bought her pretty things, like clothes, necklaces and hair ties. The boy's presents were much better! Lots of games, even a bow and arrow!

And her parents gave her the most beautiful dream-catcher. "We hope you like it Ally. Bobby has one as well and it has stopped his dreams, so we thought this one might help you."

I looked at Boris and Felix, their eyes lit up. Did Ally's parents have any idea of what could happen with a dream-catcher!!!!

"Thanks Mom and Dad, that is awesome! I love it!" she gushed.

Then her head twitched and she narrowed her eyes. "Did anyone see something blue in my dream-catcher?" Ally asked.

I hope you enjoyed reading about Bobby, Boris and Felix. Could you please assist me by leaving a review?
Thank you for your help.

Kaz x

P.s. A new Monster Adventure will be out soon.

Check out our new website...

www.bestsellingbooksforkids.com

Some other books you'll love:

Printed in Great Britain
by Amazon